Written by
Roberto Diaz

Illustrations by
David Carles

Published by

Small Books for
Big Imaginations

www.olasbooks.com
(800) 218-5302

Copyright ©2009 by Olas Enterprises, Inc., A California Corporation
PO Box 919 Dana Point, CA 92629

ISBN 0 9764788 0 3

Library of Congress Control Number: 2008910694

What's up boys and girls?
How do you do?
Let us introduce ourselves to you.

Yo, I'm Moe and I'm 11 years old
- I'm born in California
- Love to surf with my Dad
- Don't listen well
- Love Ice Cream
- *Judo Air* is my favorite trick
- I practice pickin' up 3

Hi, I'm Lani and I'm 10
- I'm born in Hawaii
- Speak English and Hawaiian
- Great Hula Dancer
- Expert problem solver
- Volunteer at Surfrider Foundation
- Love downhill carving on my Sector 9

Hola, I'm Cruz and I'm 5
- Chihuahua Skateboard Champ
- Love food
- Don't ever pull my tail!
- Like giving kisses
- *Tail Grab* is my fav trick
- Love to joke around

Can you guess Cruz's favorite food?
Do you know how to avoid a trip to the emergency room?

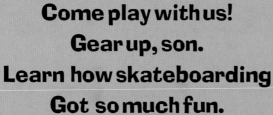

Come play with us!
Gear up, son.
Learn how skateboarding
Got so much fun.

*Notice that Moe's dad is not wearing a helmet.
Even parents sometimes forget about safety!

Let me tell you a story
how it naturally grew
in Southern California
with the surfers' crew.

with no waves to be found
and no fun games to play...

an idea came up:

We can use our boards
to roll down a hill,
Cruzie will love it
and we'll have a thrill!

"Let's cut a wooden plank-
on the bottom put some wheels."

"Take them from my skates-
yeah, check out how it feels!"

**Then a nasty fall happened
when a boy tried to shred.**

Helmets and pads
began to be used.
No need to worry now!
Bodies aren't being abused.

showing their smarts
to their moms and dads.

And on occasion
when friends may remark,
"Dude, you sure look silly
wearing pads at the park!"

Hopefully, it won't
but more likely it will:
The words come back to haunt them
when they take a nasty spill.

So, our foolish friend had to go to see a doctor,
got stitches and like 6 shots on his backside!
Is not wearing pads worth going to the hospital and being in pain??
The choice is yours, my friend!

Here are some tips for you:

1. Being safe is just as important as having fun.

2. Always, and I mean always, wear your helmet and pads.

3. Learn how to stop before you ride!

4. Skate in safe areas!

Your choices: Wear a helmet and pads = **Fun**
Don't wear your helmet and pads = **Emergency room or worse!**
A helmet can **save your life**!

Did you know that the trash in our streets and skate parks pollute our rivers and end up in our oceans?

Let's take care of our playground together! Like my friend Cobi says
PICK UP 3 WHERE EVER YOU GO.

You can help our planet and ocean by picking up your trash plus 3 more pieces.
If everyone did this, we can heal our planet!

Watch from **Sea to Summit** and check out what **TONY HAWK** says
about skateboarding and trash.

Also available

Once Upon A Wave
A Surf Story

Written by
Roberto Diaz

Paintings By
Howard Kirk

My Surf Tricks
Small Books for Big Imaginations

Written by Roberto Diaz
Paintings by Karen Adams

"It's the best thing ever, golden!"
~Rob Machado

My Surf Lesson
Look Before You Leap

Small Books for Big Imaginations

and My Surf Lesson
Coloring Book!

Young Surfer T-shirts!
by Olas

Find them at your favorite retailer, order online at
www.olasbooks.com, or call toll free **800.218.5302**

Available in organic cotton and sweatshop free t-shirts.